Big Birthday

Kate Hosford

illustrations by
**Holly
Clifton-Brown**

Carolrhoda Books / Minneapolis

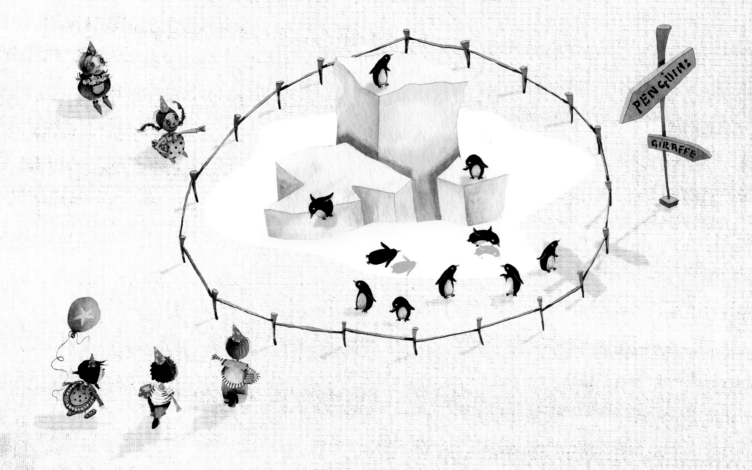

Carolrhoda Books
A division of Lerner Publishing Group, Inc.
241 First Avenue North
Minneapolis, MN 55401 USA

Website address: www.lernerbooks.com

Main body text set in April 30/30.
Typeface provided by The Font Company

Library of Congress Cataloging-in-Publication Data

Hosford, Kate.
    Big birthday / by Kate Hosford ; illustrations by Holly Clifton-Brown.
        p.   cm.
    Summary: Tired of the usual birthday parties with magicians and pizza, Annabelle decides to take her guests for a party on the moon, but problems begin before they even arrive.
    ISBN 978—0—7613—5410—9 (lib. bdg. : alk. paper)
    [1. Stories in rhyme. 2. Birthdays—Fiction. 3. Parties—Fiction. 4. Spaceflight to the moon—Fiction.
5. Individuality—Fiction. 6. Moon—Fiction.] I. Clifton-Brown, Holly, ill. II. Title.
PZ8.3.H7878Bh 2012
[E]—dc22   2011021843

Manufactured in the United States of America
1 — BC — 12/31/11

To Chris —K.H.

To Mini Holly and Sophie —H.C.-B.

Annabelle was tired of birthdays at the zoo.
She yawned at the monkeys and the baby kangaroo.

"This zoo," she announced, "is really quite a bore. I've been coming here for birthdays since I was four.

EXIT

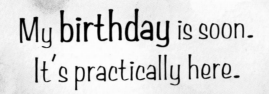

My **birthday** is soon.
It's practically here.

I think I'll have my party
on the **moon** this year."

"Oh please, Dad, please? It would be so cool!"

"I don't know," Dad said. "We'd need a lot of fuel. We could find a magician with a rabbit in his hat."

"A magician with a rabbit? Lots of parties have that!"

"Your friends could make a pizza, then decorate the cake."
"A plain old pizza party? Dad, give me a break!"

"I'll just build a spaceship. How hard can it be?
I'll fly all my friends to the **moon** with me."

She built a mighty rocket ship,
strong and airtight.
Then she painted on the outside
in lavender and white.

She made a shiny
engine from parts
that she found.

But her rocket wouldn't even rise an inch from the ground.

10 9 8 7 6 5 4 3 2

"My rocket isn't working! This is really bad! Please, do you think you could help me, Dad?

Once we get to the moon, it will be so exciting."

9 8 7 6 5 4 3

"Very well," Dad replied, "tell your friends—start inviting."

They hired out an astronaut,
experienced and smart,
Who rented them a rocket ship,
guaranteed to start.

Three, two, one—blast off!

They shot into space
with gravity pulling on
everyone's face.

They seemed to grow lighter
as they flew out of sight.
The kids flipped and floated
and played games all night.

But two days of
travel were more
than enough.

"We're tired," said the children,
"and these games are too tough."

Even Mom and Dad were
starting to despair.
"Look!" exclaimed Annabelle.
"We're almost there!"

They burst from the rocket ship
and bounced on the moon.

"Friends," said Annabelle,
"the party's starting soon!"

Mom began muttering, "Something's not right. I can't seem to get these candles to light.

We'll just sing **happy birthday** and then cut the cake."

"Mom!" whispered Annabelle. "We've made a big mistake.

The guests are getting hungry. They could really use a treat.
But if we're wearing helmets, it's impossible to eat!"

"Don't worry," Dad said,
"cake and ice cream can wait.

Everybody boogied in a cloud of moondust.

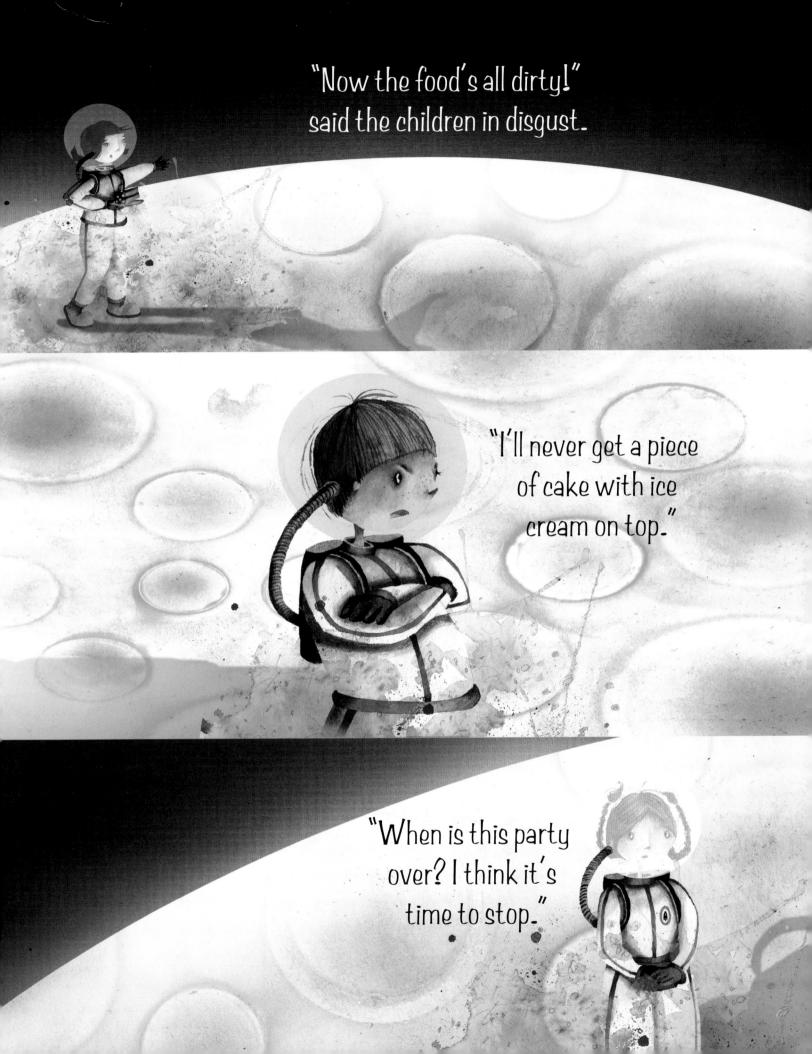

Annabelle panicked but recovered with a smile.

"Get the presents!" she directed. "We can stack them in a pile."

She opened several bracelets and a new game of chess.

But her favorite gift was a polka-dotted dress.

"It's gorgeous!" said her mother. "And it's perfect for you."

But when she tried to slip it on, she ripped it right in two!

Everyone stared at the dress that she tore. Then Annabelle just couldn't take it anymore.

"My birthday," she cried, "has become a big mess. I'm not having any fun, and neither are my guests!

My party's a disaster. I just can't stand it! I want to go home to my own cozy planet!"

They bounced into the rocket ship and sped by the stars. The children looked for Mercury, Jupiter, and Mars.

"Next year," said Annabelle, "I know what I'll do. Something really special. Something brand new."

So on her next
birthday, her friends
took a trip
on Annabelle's
very own

purple pirate ship.

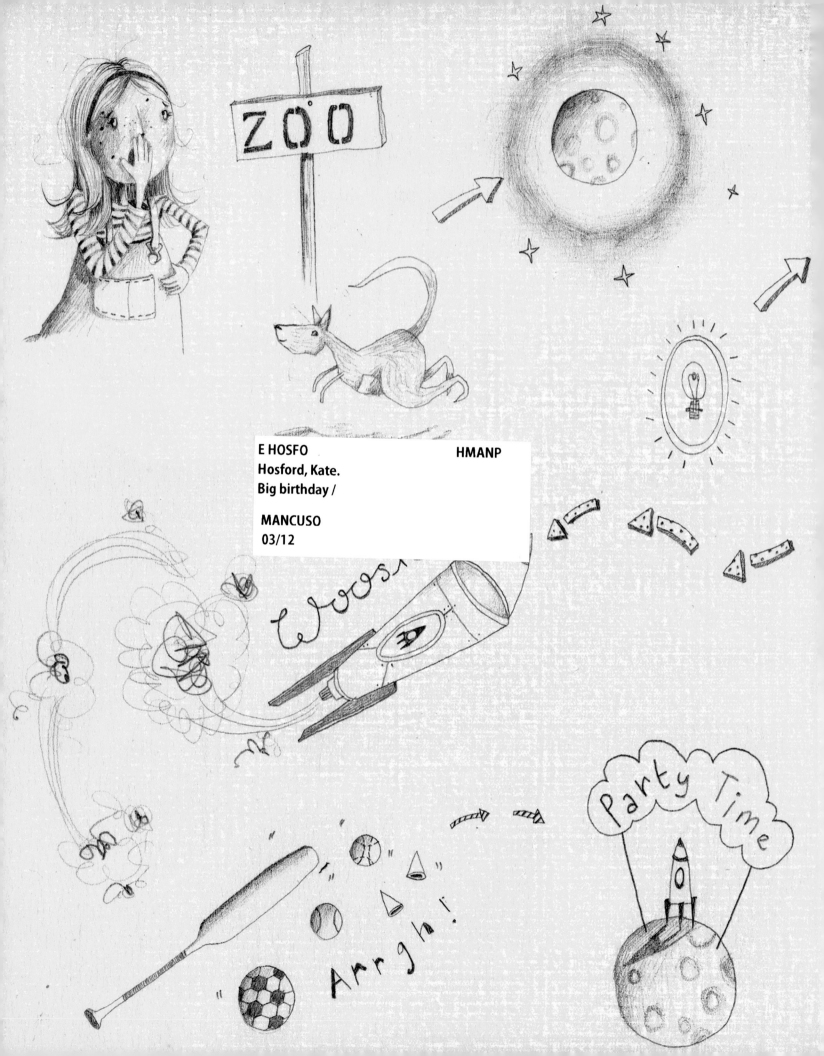